FINNEY COUNTY PUBLIC LIBRARY
605 E. Walnut
Garden City, KS 67846

P9-DNR-824

JUST FISHING WITH GRANDMA

BY GINA AND MERCER MAYER

To Zeb,
the greatest fisherman
there ever was!

A GOLDEN BOOK · NEW YORK

Just Fishing with Grandma book, characters, text, and images © 2003 Gina and Mercer Mayer.
LITTLE CRITTER, MERCER MAYER'S LITTLE CRITTER, and MERCER MAYER'S LITTLE CRITTER and Logo are
registered trademarks of Orchard House Licensing Company. All rights reserved under
International and Pan-American Copyright Conventions. Published in the United States by
Golden Books, an imprint of Random House Children's Books, a division of Random House, Inc.,
New York, and simultaneously in Canada by Random House of Canada Limited, Toronto. Golden
Books, A Golden Book, and the G colophon are registered trademarks of Random House, Inc.
Library of Congress Control Number: 2002092691
ISBN 0-307-10453-2
www.goldenbooks.com
Printed in the United States of America   First Edition 2003
10 9 8 7 6 5 4 3 2 1

I woke up this morning and thought, "What a good day to go fishing."

I asked my dad to take me fishing. But he couldn't take me today. He had to fix the car.

So I asked my mom to take me fishing, but she couldn't. She had to take my little sister to the dentist.

So I asked my grandpa to take me fishing. He couldn't take me today, either. He had to weed the garden.

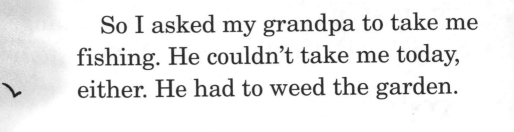

I was mad. "I guess nobody can take me fishing," I said.

Grandma said, "I'll take you fishing." So I said, "Cool! Let's go, Grandma."

FINNEY COUNTY PUBLIC LIBRARY
605 E. Walnut
Garden City, KS 67846

We got out the fishing poles, but they were just a little tangled up.

"We need worms, Grandma,"
I said. "Let's dig."
We dug here. No worms.

We dug there. No worms.

Grandma said,
"I have an idea."

We drove to the bait and tackle store.
We bought a big container of worms.

For a special treat, Grandma bought a new rod and reel for me, since the others were all messed up.

Then we drove to Lake Pookatookee.
We found a great place to fish.

Grandma helped me put a worm on my hook. I know how, though. Grandma was just afraid I might stick myself.

Our fishing lines kept getting tangled in the tree branches. And besides, we weren't catching any fish!

I noticed that all the fish were jumping
way out in the middle of the lake. "We
need a canoe, Grandma, please," I said.
Grandma rented a canoe.

Finally, we were out with the big fish.
Fish were jumping everywhere.

I caught a big one, but I guess I
wasn't holding on tight enough, because
that fish stole my new rod and reel.

I didn't even cry, but Grandma let me use hers. Then a big dark cloud covered the sky.

It started to rain. It rained hard.
"But we can't leave now," I said.
"We haven't caught any fish!"

By the time we paddled to shore, the rain had stopped, but we were both soaking wet.

We went to the snack bar and ordered their special fish fillet sandwich with wiggly fries. And you know what?

We had a great time fishing,
just Grandma and me!